Extra Innings
The Boozy Book Club Series
By
Rose Bak

Table of Contents

Chapter One – Agnes 1

Chapter Two – Nolan 5

Chapter Three – Agnes 10

Chapter Four - Nolan 14

Chapter Five - Agnes 18

Chapter Six - Nolan 25

Chapter Seven - Agnes 29

Chapter Eight - Nolan 33

Chapter Nine - Agnes 37

Chapter Ten - Nolan 41

Chapter Eleven - Agnes 46

Chapter Twelve - Nolan 50

Chapter Thirteen - Agnes 55

Chapter Fourteen - Nolan 60

Epilogue - Agnes 63

Special Preview 65

Other Books by Rose Bak 68

About the Author 71

Copyright

EXTRA INNINGS

© 2023 by Rose Bak

ALL RIGHTS RESERVED. No portion of this book may be reproduced, transmitted, downloaded, decompiled, reverse engineered, or stored in or introduced into any information storage retrieval system in any form by any means without express permission from the publisher, except as permitted by U.S. copyright law. For permissions contact the publisher at rosebakenterprises@msn.com.

Warning: the unauthorized reproduction or distribution of this copyrighted work is illegal. Criminal copyright infringement, including infringement without monetary gain, is investigated by the FBI and is punishable by up to 5 years in prison and a fine of $250,000.

This is a work of fiction. Names, characters, places, and incidents are either the product of the author's imagination or are used fictitiously. Any resemblance to actual persons, living or dead, events, organizations, or locals is entirely coincidental. Trademark names are used editorially with no infringement of the respective owner's trademark. All activities depicted occur between consenting characters 18 years or older who are not blood related.

Cover by Paper or Pixels[1]

---

1. https://paperorpixels.com/

About Extra Innings

The hunky baseball player has his eye on her, but she knows better than to trust an athlete!

Agnes always promised herself to avoid athletes at all costs. The daughter of a hockey player as famous for his philandering ways as his skill on the ice, she learned the hard way that men can't be trusted. So when she meets a hot younger man who happens to be a Triple A team pitcher, she's ready to run the other way.

Nolan loves three things: baseball, his mama, and the PR executive who's working with him to bring more publicity to his baseball team. Sure, she's a little older than him, a little prickly, and she thinks his beloved sport is "ridiculous", but he's a patient man. He's going to approach her like he's approached his career: with intense focus, persistence, and a little bit of strategy.

This seventh inning stretch is going to lead to love.

"Extra Innings" is part of the "Boozy Book Club" series. Each story in the series is a steamy standalone featuring a couple in their forties and fifties, a nosy group of book club friends, a little bit of humor, and a sweet happily ever after that proves anyone can find love later in life.

Join My Mailing List

Join Rose Bak's mailing list at bit.ly/RoseBakNewsletter[2]. You'll get a free book and be the first to hear about all the latest releases and special sales.

Dedication

In memory of those first warm summer days in the nineteen nineties where young Chicago professionals played hooky, sat in the bleachers at Wrigley Field, drank beer, ate hotdogs, and did the "Seventh Inning Stretch" with Harry Caray. Those were the days, my friends.

Chapter One – Agnes

"Welcome back to the Boozy Book Club."

I smiled at Evie, the owner of Boozy Books and organizer of the book club, as she greeted me at the door.

"Hey Evie, I was out of town for a couple of weeks, then catching up on work, but I'm glad to be back."

Evie's face softened in sympathy. "I heard about your mother Agnes, I'm so sorry for your loss."

I wasn't surprised that Evie had heard. This was a small town and even though I was a relative newcomer, having moved here only five years ago, people still seemed to know a surprising amount of information about my life.

"Thank you. I'm just grateful she passed peacefully."

My sisters and I had been shocked when our mother had literally dropped dead in the middle of the meat aisle at the Piggly Wiggly. We hadn't done an autopsy, but the doctors were fairly sure it had been a heart attack. Mama had spent a lot of time in that meat aisle, and other than the occasional cob of sweet corn, she'd never been much for vegetables. Still, it was a shock to lose my mother when I was only forty-three years old.

Funny how forty-three used to seem old, but now that I was there, I'd added the "only" as a prefix.

I joined a few of my friends at one of the tables and we started discussing this month's book. The Boozy Book Club was unusual for two reasons. First, it paired alcoholic drinks with the book of the month. Second, one by one all of the book club members seemed to be finding love, despite the fact we were all in our forties and fifties. Weirder still, the books we read somehow seemed to predict the kind of man who'd turn up and sweep one of us off our feet.

When we read a billionaire romance, one of the ladies fell for a local billionaire. When we'd read about a biker who accidentally impregnated his lady love, the same thing happened to another woman in the club. Even Evie wasn't immune. When we read a mystery book, she'd fallen in love with the cop who was investigating some mysterious break-ins at the bookstore. I hadn't been there, but I'd heard that a couple of months ago our newest member was carried off by a firefighter – right after everyone read a book about a firefighter.

It was crazy, and yet every month another one of our members found unexpected love.

Needless to say, our membership numbers had been growing as every lonely single woman in the county came hoping to be the lucky one who'd find love this month. I wasn't interested in falling in love – though I guess I wouldn't be opposed to it if it happened to come along – I was here for the books. And the booze.

"Ladies, may I have your attention please."

We all looked at Evie expectantly.

"I hope y'all enjoyed this month's selection. I'm betting that you're really going to like our theme for next month. In honor of Spring Training, next month's theme is 'Baseball and Beer'. We'll be reading a baseball romance called "Extra Innings" and sampling a selection of local craft beers. As always, the book is available for purchase downstairs or in our online store. See you next month."

"In honor of spring training?" I looked at my friend Tara. "It's February."

"Spring training starts the last week of February," she explained.

I shook my head. "Sports ball is weird."

She rolled her eyes. "Sports ball? I guess we know which one of us *won't* find love with a baseball player this month."

Tara's words came back to me a few days later. My boss called me into his office early one morning to let me know he'd selected me for a new assignment. I worked at a public relations firm, mostly doing social media campaigns, press releases, and branded content.

"Agnes, thanks for coming. I need your help on a project."

"Sure John, what do you need?"

"We're partnering with the Bay City Seagulls to overhaul their social media. I'd like you to take the lead. I need my best person on this project."

"The Bay City what now?" I asked in confusion.

"Our Triple A baseball team."

At my lack of comprehension he added, "Minor league baseball? The gateway to the majors?"

"I don't know anything about baseball."

"Don't worry, you'll figure it out eventually."

I doubted I would, but I didn't want to disappoint my boss. He'd been kind after my mama had passed, offering me a longer bereavement leave than company policy dictated. Plus, I was hoping to get a promotion when one of the directors left. I really liked this firm and was hoping to stay here for many years.

"It's a three month contract over the preseason," John continued. "If they are happy with our performance, they promised to offer us a multi-year contract, so I don't have to tell you how important this is to the firm. A big client like the Gulls could lead to a whole new business line in professional sports."

No pressure Agnes, none at all, I thought to myself.

"Don't worry Agnes, I have full confidence in you," he added, clearly reading my expression. "You excel at these kinds of projects."

"Who's my contact?" I asked. "I'll start doing some research on the organization."

"You'll be working with the Chief Administrative Officer, Liz McNally. I'll email you her contact information and a copy of our temporary contract with the Seagulls so you can get started. Let me know if you need anything."

As I walked out of John's office, I couldn't help but shake my head at the irony. Me, the person who knew nothing about professional sports other than she hated athletes, was about to spend the next couple of months trying to make those arrogant jerks look good. Somewhere from the bowels of hell, or maybe a mansion in Minnesota somewhere, my no good daddy was laughing.

Chapter Two – Nolan

"How's your shoulder Nolan?"

I tried not to grimace as our trainer Franklin pressed around the overused muscles. I'd just pitched a no-hitter, but right now, I was feeling every single one of my thirty-five years.

"Fine, I just need to ice it."

Franklin looked skeptical but didn't comment, instead heading over to the freezer to grab some ice packs. I heard the tip tap of high heeled shoes and turned to find our Chief Administrative Officer heading my way.

"Hey Liz."

"Hi Nolan, great game today."

"Thanks." When she continued to stand there looking at me I added, "Did you need something?"

"I've got a community engagement assignment for you."

I repressed a sigh. Liz's community engagement assignments were notoriously sucky. Last time some of my teammates and I got stuck teaching a group of seniors how to play baseball at the community center. We spent the entire day getting our asses pinched and our biceps fondled by dirty-minded octogenarians. I still had nightmares about it. But I was a team player, so I wasn't going to argue about it.

"Whatcha got for me?"

"The club has engaged a new public relations firm, a local one this time. Those national assholes were useless."

Liz's father was the team owner and after being around baseball players her whole life she'd developed the mouth of a sailor.

"What's that have to do with me?"

"We decided we wanted to revamp our social media presence, and also do a publicity series based on the player's view of the game," Liz explained. "There will be social media posts highlighting the parts of the stadium people don't normally see, candid shots of the players in the community, human interest stories on the players, that kind of thing. We're hoping it will help bolster attendance, which as you know, has been lagging the last couple of seasons since we came back from the pandemic lockdowns. You've been selected to be the player liaison to the PR person."

I groaned. "Why me?"

"You're the oldest player on the team, and the least likely to do something stupid."

"Gee thanks."

"Plus, it's your last year. You're going to need to get used to doing this kind of thing for your new job."

After this season, I was hanging up my cleats and moving to management. The Seagulls had offered me a position as their new scout. Our current scout, Buzz Henderson, had been sourcing talent for the club for thirty years, but his wife was fed up with all the traveling and after a health scare over Christmas, he was ready to live a life of leisure. At least I knew what I was doing when I retired from baseball, which put me way ahead of most guys who were staring down at the end of their playing days.

"After you're done icing and showering, why don't you come up to my office. Agnes Scott is meeting us there at four o'clock."

"Got it."

An hour later I arrived at Liz's office, freshly showered and pumped up with anti-inflammatories. I rapped my knuckles on the door, not waiting for permission to enter. We were pretty informal here. Liz was sitting at the table with a woman, the PR lady I presumed.

The woman stood up and I had a quick impression of a plump ass and sharp shoulders before she turned around. With a name like Agnes, I'd expected a seventy year old woman. This woman appeared to be firmly in her late thirties or early forties, judging by the fine lines bracketing her dark brown eyes and the slight softening around her jaw.

She had light brown hair that was pulled back into a low ponytail, bringing her sharp cheekbones into stark relief. My eyes skimmed her cupid's bow mouth before taking in large breasts, an indented waist, curvy hips, and long, lean legs that peeked out from beneath her knee-length skirt.

Agnes was rounded, womanly, and...mine. I jolted back as that thought popped into my head. What the hell was that?

"Mr. Jacobs? I'm Agnes Scott, it's nice to meet you."

When I stood there looking at her like a dolt, she stepped forward to shake my hand. My fingers moved to hers, purely out of muscle memory. The spark between our palms jolted me back to my senses. I saw her glance at our hands with a brief look of puzzlement, telling me she felt it too.

"Nice to meet you," I said gruffly. "Shall we get started?"

We all sat down at the table while I tried to figure out what was going on with me. Had I gotten hit in the head with a ball? No, I would have remembered that. At least I thought I would.

"You okay Nolan?" Liz asked.

"Oh yeah, fine."

"Agnes why don't you tell us what the plan is?"

I hoped she was going to say to spend the rest of her life with me. Instead, she said, "I'd like to spend some time getting some pictures and anecdotes from around the stadium, a behind the scenes look at the turf and whatever is inside the building."

"Field," I corrected.

"Excuse me?"

"It's called the field, not the turf."

Her expression didn't change, but I had the distinct impression that Agnes was rolling her eyes at me. "Got it."

"Nolan, we'd like you to spend some time with Agnes, show her around the stadium, and introduce her to the players."

"You should come for one of our games this week too," I suggested.

"Oh, no, that's all right, I don't need to watch a game."

"Sure you do," I replied, unsure of why I was arguing with her other than I really wanted her to be around me as much as possible. "Have you ever seen us play?"

"I've never been to any baseball games," Agnes said.

"Never? Not even in high school or college?" When she shook her head I asked, "Little League?"

Another head shake. "So, you're what? A football fan? Basketball? Soccer?"

"I don't follow sports," she said, her voice firm enough to make me suspect there was more to the story than her simple statement. "Any sports. I'm not a fan."

As if remembering that she'd just accepted a contract working for a sports team, her eyes widened slightly.

"I don't need to like the game to do a good job promoting it," she assured Liz. "I've promoted many things that I found to be ridiculous."

"You think baseball is ridiculous?" I asked incredulously. "It's America's game."

"Okay," she said, her tone placating like I was a toddler having a tantrum. "I promise you we'll get the spirit of the game and its players captured for this campaign. Let me show you some of my initial ideas."

Agnes spent the next twenty minutes outlining her ideas for the campaign, occasionally flipping her laptop around to show us examples on her computer screen. I had to admit that I was impressed. I didn't know a damn thing about marketing, but I could easily see how her ideas would translate to the game and our team in particular.

"When should we get started?" I asked as she wrapped up.

She turned on her phone, navigating to her calendar. She bit her lower lip as she squinted at the calendar, a line furrowing between her brows. It was adorable.

"How does tomorrow afternoon look?" she asked.

I didn't need to look. I had the team's schedule burned into my brain after all these years.

"Tomorrow afternoon works. Say around two o'clock?" I suggested. "I can meet you at the player's entrance and let you in."

She tapped on her phone screen, inputting the appointment. "Fine, I'll see you then."

Chapter Three – Agnes

I couldn't say why I spent the rest of the day thinking about Nolan. There was something about him that I couldn't get out of my mind.

It wasn't just that he was attractive – God knows he was – but it was more about this weird kind of magnetism that made me want to attach myself to him. It was ridiculous. The man was a professional athlete, and several years younger than me. He was probably the type of guy who had groupies, or whatever they called them in sports, around him at all times. I could picture him surrounded by a bunch of young bottle blondes with huge breasts staring at him adoringly. Yuk.

He might be young, but he had a rugged attractiveness to him. He had piercing green eyes, dark auburn hair, and a matching beard. I'd never been a fan of beards, but I couldn't help but wonder how Nolan's facial hair would feel scraping against my inner thighs.

Like most baseball players I'd seen, Nolan had massive biceps, strong shoulders, and an impressively muscled ass. I felt the strongest desire to squeeze those round globes. I closed my eyes and chastised myself at my ridiculousness, but that just made me remember the look on Nolan's face when I called baseball ridiculous. He'd looked like I'd insulted his mother while running over his dog. It was endearing.

I sighed deeply. I was a grown woman, there was no way I was going to have a crush on a younger man, and an athlete at that. My mother had been married to an athlete for about ten years.

Daddy played hockey in the NHL, and he spent most of his time traveling around, returning home a few times a year to send our lives into upheaval. He and my mama had been on and off again for several years until she'd seen his face in the tabloids one too many times and sent him packing. He'd insisted on visitation rights with us three girls, but it had just been a way to get back at Mama for having the nerve to divorce him. We didn't see hide nor hair of him for years after the divorce.

After that experience, there was one thing my mama and my sisters and I could all agree on: no dating athletes. Ever. They couldn't be trusted.

Daddy hadn't bothered to show up at Mama's funeral either, even though my youngest sister had sent word that she'd passed. She'd had to do that through his agent, since none of us even had his phone number or e-mail.

I shook my head. Why was I even thinking about dating athletes? Damn Evie and her book club for sending my mind into a direction that it had no reason going.

"You look like you're in deep thought." I started at the voice coming from right in front of me.

"Oh, Nolan, you scared me," I said, placing a hand over my pounding heart. His eyes darkened as he eyed my chest. I tore my hand away like it had burned me.

"Are you ready to get started?" I asked.

Nolan nodded. "I thought we could start with a tour of the parts of the stadium the fans don't get to see."

"Sounds good."

We spent the next hour poking around the bowels of the Seagulls stadium, taking pictures and making notes about things that would be good for the PR campaign. As we walked through the mostly deserted building, occasionally Nolan's hand or shoulder would brush against mine, setting off a chain reaction of excited quivers and dampened panties. It was ridiculous, especially at my age, but no matter how sternly I told myself to knock it off, I couldn't help the attraction I was feeling for him.

When we got to the team locker room, I pulled to a stop.

"There's not going to be any naked men in there, is there?" I asked.

He gave me a smirk, something I'd learned was his default expression. "You got something against naked men?"

"There's a time and a place for nakedness," I said primly.

Nolan's eyes darted to my chest again before returning to my face. I made a mental note to go back to that lingerie boutique downtown and buy a few more bras like the one I was wearing. Clearly it was working for me.

"No one should be here," Nolan answered. "All the workouts and meetings were over a couple of hours ago."

He led me through the locker room, which smelled just about as bad as I'd expected, showing me the rooms where they met with the trainers for ice baths, massage, and other bodywork.

"This here is my locker," he told me, tapping on a green metal door as we passed.

"Hold up, let's do a 'what's in Nolan's locker' video."

He gave me a skeptical look but complied. I opened the video app on my phone, then stepped back to frame the shot.

"Just pretend we're having a conversation," I instructed. "Look at me when you talk. And don't worry if you mess up, I'll edit this later."

"Got it."

"We're here in the Bay City Seagulls locker room with Nolan Jacobs who plays, um..." I stopped awkwardly, drawing a blank.

"I'm the pitcher." The smirk was back. I pressed my thighs together.

"The pitcher for the Bay City Seagulls. Nolan why don't you tell us about what's in your locker?"

I zoomed in on the neat stacks inside. Nolan raised one eyebrow but complied with my request.

"Well let's see here, I've got deodorant, a comb, a jockstrap, my cup..."

I felt my face flame as he held up his protective gear. I wasn't an expert in this particular area, but it looked larger than I'd expected.

"Gotta protect the family jewels," he winked, as if sensing my embarrassment.

"Let's keep this family friendly," I snapped.

"Understood."

He took out something that looked like a rabbit's foot.

"What's that?"

"This is my good luck charm that I got in Little League from my godfather, Nolan Ryan."

"That's sweet. Was he your coach? Or just a Little League fan?"

Nolan's jaw dropped. "You don't know who Nolan Ryan is?"

"You just told me. He's your godfather."

"Oh. My. God. You were serious. You really don't know anything about baseball at all, do you?" He looked appalled.

I stopped recording and frowned at him. "This isn't about me, it's about getting publicity from the team."

"Nolan Ryan was one of the greatest baseball players of our time. He was teammates with my father when they both played for the Astros," Nolan continued.

"That's nice," I said politely. "Can we continue with the interview now?"

Nolan's expression turned grouchy.

"No ma'am, this is not going to do. What are you doing tonight?"

"Nothing, why?"

"You're going to come over to my place and get a baseball tutorial."

"No, I'm not. First of all, I don't even know you. Second of all, I have no interest in learning about baseball or any other stupid sport. I hate sports."

Chapter Four - Nolan

I couldn't believe my ears. How could the woman of my dreams hate sports? And she really was the woman of my dreams, I'd become more and more convinced of it as the day went on. I just needed to convince Agnes of that little fact.

She wasn't immune to me, I was sure of that. Every time we brushed against each other she'd let out this soft little exhale that made my dick twitch. And when I was close to her, like I was right now, I could see her pulse hammering furiously in her neck.

"Okay how about this? We'll go to a sports bar and watch the Braves game together there instead."

"Did you miss the part about me hating sports?" she asked.

"You told me yourself, you don't know the first thing about baseball. How can you proclaim to hate something you know nothing about?"

She opened her mouth, set to argue with me I'm sure, but I interrupted her.

"I bet your boss would like you to have at least some idea what you're promoting. Besides, you can get some insight into baseball fans since there's usually a bunch of them in the bar on game nights."

"You're pulling the boss card on me?" she asked incredulously.

"Would it help if I told you the bar has the best burger you've tasted in your entire life?"

I could see her wavering. "How are their fries?"

"Which kind? Regular, sweet potato, or chili?"

She looked intrigued, and that's when I knew I had her.

"If I watch one game with you, will you stop trying to convince me to like baseball?"

"Yes ma'am," I lied.

"Fine," she huffed. "When and where am I meeting you?"

A few hours later I was set up at a table waiting for Agnes to come in. I'd chosen the perfect table where we could easily see the game on one of two large screens on either side of the room. While I waited, I frantically rehearsed scenarios where I tried to get to know Agnes with varying degrees of success. I was so distracted that I didn't notice her come in until she was almost to the table.

My eyes widened as I took her in. Her light brown hair was down, hanging around her face and brushing the tops of her shoulders. She was wearing a form-fitting long-sleeve shirt in some sort of dark pink, faded jeans, and a pair of black converse sneakers. She looked adorable.

"What?" she said, growing uncomfortable under my perusal. "You told me to dress comfortably and casual."

"That I did," I said, pointing to my own jeans and dark green Henley. I'd worn it on purpose on account of how multiple women had told me that the color brought out the green in my eyes. If I wanted to get Agnes to notice me, I needed to use every tool in my arsenal.

"Have a seat," I said, pulling out a chair. She nodded her thanks as she sat down.

I sat across from her, and our eyes caught and held. It felt like there was some invisible connection drawing us together.

"You want something to drink?" The waitress came by, breaking the spell, and we each ordered a drink: club soda for me and a diet coke for Agnes.

"I would have thought you'd order a beer," she remarked.

"I don't usually drink during the season, especially the day before a game."

"It's a long season, isn't it?"

"Yep, about nine months," I answered.

"How long have you been with the team?" she asked.

"I played for the Gulls for two years, then I got called up to Atlanta for ten years, and now this is my second season back with the Gulls. And my last. I'm retiring after this year."

"Retire? You're only thirty-five," she protested.

"That's ancient for a baseball player."

My eyes moved to the television as I saw the pitcher head to the mound. The leadoff man started swinging his bat, loosening up his shoulder.

"The game is fixing to start. Let's talk baseball. There are nine innings of play..."

I spent the next couple of hours alternating between doing my Baseball 101 spiel and trying to pry information out of Agnes. Unfortunately, the woman was a vault, always turning the conversation back to things related to her PR campaign for the team.

As we watched the game, we ate burgers with salad, shared a basket of fries, and found one common interest: people watching. During one of the commercial breaks Agnes nodded to a couple sitting at a table along the wall.

"Oh look, those two are on their first date."

I craned my neck to follow her line of vision. "How do you know?"

"See how she's a bit stiff, like she's not sure if she's comfortable? There are halting breaks in their conversation. And his body language is like a peacock, preening for her."

"You don't know that," I scoffed. "There's no way to tell they're on a date just from seeing them across the room."

Her face turned stubborn.

"Oh yeah? You want to bet? Come on."

Agnes stood up, grabbing my hand, and pulling me alongside her as she moved towards the couple's table. They both looked up as we approached, and I offered the woman a non-threatening smile.

"Excuse me," Agnes said sweetly, her attention fixed on the woman. "Do you mind settling a bet for us?"

The man looked slightly irritated, but the woman was game. "Sure."

"How long have you been dating?" Agnes asked. "You are dating, right?"

"Kind of. This is actually our first date."

Agnes elbowed me in the gut. "See? I told you."

Just then recognition lit up in the guy's eyes. "Hey wait, you're Nolan Jacobs aren't you?"

"Yes I am."

"I'm a big fan," he said enthusiastically. "Susie, this is Nolan Jacobs the pitcher for the Gulls."

The woman looked about as impressed as Agnes had been when she met me. She was clearly not into the sport. These women were hell on the ego.

"Do you mind if I get a selfie?" the guy asked.

"Sure," I said. I bet I'd taken thousands of selfies during my career.

"Let me help," Agnes said, bringing her phone out of her pocket.

I moved to the man's side as she snapped a few pictures of us, then got the man's email address.

"I'll send you copies of the photos as well as a release form—if it's okay for us to use this on our social media?" she asked the guy.

"That would be awesome! Thanks."

We left the happy fan to finish his first date and headed back to our own table.

"Well, we learned two things just now," I told Agnes. "First, you are indeed an astute observer of human behavior and second, at least some people like the Seagulls."

"Stick with me and I'll have more people clamoring to take selfies with you and come watch your baseball games."

"I think I'd like to do just that."

"What?"

"Stick with you."

Chapter Five - Agnes

There was something intense about Nolan's gaze. Pus, the way he said he wanted to stick with me sounded almost...flirty. I did a mental eye roll at my ridiculousness. The man was a professional athlete. Flirting was in their DNA.

When I didn't respond to his comment, Nolan leaned closer. "I'd like to spend more time with you Agnes. Please tell me you're single and that you'll go out with me again."

I glanced down to my bare left hand, though I couldn't say why. There had never been a ring there.

"Are you messing with me right now?" I asked, suddenly irritated.

He frowned. "What do you mean?"

"Are you just trying to give the old lady a thrill?"

My voice sounded cold, even to my own ears, probably because part of me wished he really meant what he was saying, and that just made me annoyed with myself.

"What old lady?" he asked incredulously. "You don't mean you?"

At my nod he asked, "How old are you? Thirty-six? Thirty-eight?"

"Forty-three."

"That's only eight years older than me." His tone implied it was no big deal.

"Only. Ha. Well, even if you are serious, I don't date athletes."

"I'm serious as a heart attack," he said solemnly.

He looked sincere, but my daddy had always looked sincere too – even when he'd been lying through his teeth.

"You shouldn't joke about heart problems around the middle aged."

His mouth dropped open and I repressed a smile. It was fun messing with him. I stood up, gathering my purse and jacket.

"Thanks for the baseball lesson, and for dinner. I'll see you at the stadium tomorrow."

I was only the tiniest bit sad that he didn't follow me. Then again, I didn't blame him. I'd been unnecessarily rude to him, which wasn't like me.

I sighed deeply as I turned on my car. After sending a quick text to confirm it was okay, I headed over to my friend Tara's house. Tara and I had met in a water aerobics class not long after I moved to this small town, and we'd become fast friends.

Over a bottle of wine, I recounted the story of my day including my weird conversation with Nolan at the bar and his flirting with me.

"Oh my God! You're going to be this month's book club romance." Tara looked thrilled.

"No, I'm not," I protested. "Just because we're reading a baseball book and I happened to meet a baseball player doesn't mean we're going to fall in love."

"Have you read any of the book yet?" she asked.

"No, I haven't even looked at it."

Tara got up and came back with her copy, opening it up and reading the description.

"He's a washed up baseball star. She's his best friend's daughter. Can they put aside their differences and win the grand slam...of love?"

"Good Lord, that sounds terrible. Who picked that book? A fourteen year-old girl?"

"Don't you see Agnes? A baseball player at the end of his career. An age gap. A couple from two different worlds. It's totally you and Nolan, although you have a reverse age gap, and he's not washed up yet, although he is retiring, so that probably counts."

I shook my head at my normally practical friend. "You have totally lost it. That doesn't sound anything like me and Nolan. What has gotten into you?"

Tara set the book down with a dreamy expression. "I wonder if one of the book club books will bring me love?"

"We are way too old for this romantic nonsense," I said firmly. "The book club does not control our romantic fate."

"I've been divorced for eight years," Tara reminded me. "I don't want to die alone. I need a book club hero of my own."

I sighed. "Thanks for confirming for me how ridiculous it is for me to be attracted to Nolan."

"Oh, so you admit that you're attracted to him?" Tara's eyebrows rose towards her hairline.

"Of course I'm attracted to him, Tara. I'm a heterosexual woman with eyeballs in her head, aren't I?"

"And he's a heterosexual man with eyeballs in his head too. Maybe you can trust him when he says he's attracted to you."

"Maybe you can never trust an athlete," I said stubbornly.

She opened her mouth to respond but I interrupted her. "I've got to go home. Thanks for listening. I'll talk to you later."

The next week I spent a lot of time out at the ballpark. I had several other accounts to work on, but this one was big enough that my boss had reminded me repeatedly that I should prioritize the Seagulls in the hope that my work would make us attractive to some of the other sports teams in the region. Lucky me, getting to be the sports specialist. The way things were going, I'd wind up spending the rest of my career hanging around with athletes.

Every time I visited the ballpark I spent a lot of time with Nolan. Liz had said he was my main contact person, but even so, it didn't matter what project I was working on, or which player I was interviewing, Nolan managed to be right there, his warm eyes boring into me.

If we were around other people, his attitude towards me was friendly and neutral, but when we were alone, his voice deepened, and his tone became decidedly more flirty. He'd move just a smidge closer than he should, gifting me with little touches that drove me crazy. His knee touching mine lightly underneath a table. His shoulder bumping mine as we walked. His hand skimming my lower back as he accompanied me someplace.

And then there were the texts. Somehow he'd weaseled my phone number out of me, claiming he needed a way to contact me about our meetings. I didn't have a work cell phone, preferring to only manage one phone, so I had to give him my personal number. He took to texting me a couple of times a day, sharing baseball trivia, memes, or flirty banter.

Nolan: *I didn't see you after the game, what did you think of your first Gulls game?*

Agnes: *It was good. Liz was explaining some things to me while we watched but I never saw you batting. What happened? I didn't want to ask Liz in case you'd get in trouble.*

Nolan: *I wouldn't get in trouble. Pitchers usually don't bat, we generally use a designated hitter.*

Agnes: *Why not?*

Nolan: *We need to save our energy – and our arms – for pitching.*

Agnes: *So all the other guys play offense and defense but not you? That doesn't seem fair to the other guys who have to do both.*

Nolan: *Look at you, using sports terms, I'm so proud.*

Agnes: *Also the games are soooo looong!*

Nolan: *It teaches you stamina and patience. I'd be glad to demonstrate my stamina and patience tomorrow night at my place. [winking emoji]*

Agnes: *You're incorrigible.*

Nolan: *I think you meant incredibly sexy.*

The flirty texting was torture. I'd spent more time with my vibrator over the last few weeks than I had in the last few years. It was a good thing it plugged in, because if I relied on batteries I'd have to buy out the store.

It wasn't just physical though, I'd grown to really like Nolan as a friend too. But my feelings were too jumbled, and it was hard to separate the attraction from the friendship. I was relieved when the team went on a ten-day road trip, giving me the opportunity to detox from my little obsession with Nolan. While the team was gone, I mostly focused on my other projects.

Late Friday afternoon I was coming back from a meeting with Liz when I turned a corner and damn near ran into Nolan. His large hands came around my upper arms to keep me from falling. Running into that muscled chest was like running into a wall.

"Just the woman I've been looking for," he drawled, giving me a smile that made my lady parts tingle.

"You're back," I said inanely. "I mean, the team's back."

His eyes sparkled. "We are. Did you miss me, Agnes?"

He squeezed my biceps, reminding me that he was still holding onto me. I pulled back, but instead of letting go, Nolan slid one hand down my arm to snag my hand.

"I need to talk to you about something," he said, pulling me up the hallway and into some kind of storage closet. The shelves were filled with stacks of Seagulls swag.

"What did you—?"

My words cut off as Nolan tugged on my hand, pulling me close. He smelled good, like pine and man.

"I was thinking about this the entire time I was on the road."

Nolan's mouth descended onto mine, his soft lips pressing against my own. My eyes widened in shock even as my body said, "Yes, finally!"

I pulled back. "Nolan!"

I meant to chastise him, but then I looked into his eyes and before I could stop myself, I damn near threw myself at him. I raised up onto my tiptoes, gripping his shoulders and reaching up to capture his mouth. Nolan groaned, his arms sliding around my waist as I slid my tongue along his.

He walked me backwards until my back was pressed against the shelves. His hardness grew against my stomach, and I couldn't help rocking my pelvis against him as the kiss went on and on. I vaguely heard the shelf rattling behind me as we ground against each other like two teens dry humping in the backseat of a car.

Suddenly I felt something soft hit my head and shoulders. Some *things* soft, raining down on us, followed by a now-empty cardboard box. I looked around and saw a pile of foam on the floor around us.

"What are those?"

We were both breathing heavily as we looked at the contents of the box we'd knocked off the shelf. Nolan picked one up and pulled it over his hand, showing me a giant foam hand. One finger was pointed upwards with "We're number one!" printed on one side, and the Gulls logo on the other.

I smiled. "I don't understand the appeal of those things."

Nolan slid one foam finger up the side of my face and I shivered. He moved the foam finger down, using it to circle my breasts through my shirt, then sliding it down my belly until the foam finger notched between my legs. I gasped and smacked his arm.

"Nolan! Be good!"

He tossed the foam hand away and leaned forward to give me a quick peck on the lips, his hands braced on the shelf behind me.

"That was a fine welcome," Nolan whispered, his lips an inch away from mine.

He kissed me again, our tongues tangling, our bodies plastered together.

"We shouldn't do this," I said when we broke apart again, but even I could hear the lack of conviction in my voice. I'd never understood the appeal of drugs, but kissing Nolan was like taking a hit of…well, whatever people took a hit of. It was completely addictive.

"Why not? We're both single and obviously very attracted to each other." He pointed to the floor. "And we're number one."

I slid out from underneath his arms. Nolan turned to lean against the door, watching me as I paced across the storage room.

"I'm not one for casual sex," I told him. "That kind of stuff was okay in college, but at this age, it doesn't interest me."

"Good," he said. "I don't want a one-night stand. With you, I want more."

Forever would be good. I ignored the voice in my head.

"Also, we work together," I reminded him.

"You're a short-term consultant, I don't think we're breaking any workplace policies if we're both consenting to seeing each other."

"It doesn't matter. You're way too young for me," I said firmly. "You're practically a kid."

He rolled his eyes. "I'm a grown man. Have been for a long time."

Suddenly he looked uncertain.

"I'm not misreading the situation, am I? You're attracted to me the same way I am to you, right?"

As much as I wanted to deny it, I couldn't lie to him. Those kisses had been explosive; I'd never felt anything so powerful before.

"Yes, I'm attracted to you Nolan, and more than that, I like you as a person. You seem like a great guy. But I don't date athletes."

"So you've said. May I ask why that is?"

I shook my head. "I'd really rather not talk about it."

He stepped away from the door.

"I won't force you," he said. "But since I know you're interested, I reserve the right to pull out all the stops."

"Pull out all the stops?" I asked in confusion, wondering if this was a baseball metaphor.

He stalked forward, cupping my cheek in his palm as he looked into my eyes. "I want you Agnes. I'm going to do whatever it takes to make you change your mind."

Chapter Six - Nolan

I talked a big game about pulling out all the stops, but the fact was, I had no idea what to do to convince Agnes that I was serious about her. Those ten days on the road had been torture. Other than when I was on the field – I had trained myself to be laser focused on the game when I was playing – every other waking moment I thought of Agnes. I was like a middle school boy with a crush on his teacher.

With all my years on the road, with both the Seagulls and Atlanta, I couldn't think of one single time when I'd actually missed someone. Besides my mama, of course. I was a mama's boy, so sue me.

I knew Agnes was worried about our age difference, but she was only eight years older than me, not a lot in the scheme of things. I was also acutely aware that no one would bat an eye at the idea of a man dating a woman eight years younger than him. In fact, I knew a lot of guys my age that were dating girls in their twenties. I wasn't going to let something as insignificant as an eight-year age gap get in our way.

I spent the next week brooding about that kiss and how I could repeat it. Agnes had been MIA from the ballpark, claiming she was working on other projects, and her answers to my texts were brief and impersonal. I figured that kiss had affected her as much as it had me, and that was why she was putting up walls.

By Friday it had been a full week since I'd seen Agnes. We'd gone out of town for a short three-day road trip, and when I got back, Liz was waiting for me.

"Hey Nolan, I'd like to have you join us for the local correspondent's dinner tomorrow night. Sorry for the late notice, I forgot to ask you about it before you went out of town."

"What's the correspondence dinner?" I asked.

"It's like an awards dinner for the local press. The Seagulls buy a table every year, and my Dad selects managers to attend and sit at his table. This year, he and I agreed to invite you instead of Buzz."

"Well, that feels cold. The man's not even retired yet."

She made a face I couldn't quite interpret. "Well, the truth is that Buzz argues with us about going every year. He hates that stuff. Believe me when I say he'll be relieved when he hears we invited you instead of him. In fact, he probably would have suggested it himself if he'd thought of it."

"Well then, I guess I can go."

"Great, I'll email you the details. Wear a suit."

She started to hustle off and I put a hand on her arm. "Do I get to bring a date?"

She gave me a curious look. "I didn't realize you were dating anyone, Nolan."

"I was thinking it would be a good event to bring Agnes to, you know, so she can spend some time with your dad and the managers in a social setting."

Liz's expression turned shrewd. "You like Agnes?"

I nodded. There was no sense lying to Liz, she'd get the information out of me eventually anyway.

"Yeah, I like her a lot, and I think she likes me too. But she thinks I'm too young for her, and she says she doesn't date athletes."

"There's a story there, I bet."

"No doubt."

"I just need to find a way to spend more time with her so I can show her that we're meant to be together forever."

Liz got a sappy look on her face and sighed. "Oh my God, you really do like her, don't you? This is awesome."

"I do."

"Well, I'll tell you what, I'll get her there for you, but then you've got to do the rest."

"I sure will. How are you going to convince her?"

"She invited me to join her at some book club she's involved in, and the meeting is tonight. I'll bring it up then."

"Perfect. I appreciate your help."

"Just don't make me sorry, Nolan. You're a good friend, but Agnes is becoming a friend too. I don't have a lot of women friends, so I take the 'sisters before misters' credo very seriously."

"I promise to treat her right."

Later that night I received a text from Agnes.

Agnes: *I understand I'm your date for some fancy dinner this weekend.*

Nolan: *It'll be a good opportunity for you to get some face time with the owners and executives.*

Agnes: *Exactly what Liz said, but I'm not sure why I have to be your date to do that.*

Nolan: *Don't try to question the wisdom of Liz. I learned that long ago. It's best just to go along with it when she gets an idea in her head.*

Agnes: *I feel like this is a set-up.*

Nolan: *I'll take the fifth on that. How about I pick you up at six?*

Agnes: *I can meet you there.*

Nolan: *No ma'am, I'm a gentleman and I always pick up my dates and make sure they get home safe afterwards too.*

Agnes: *Fine.*

Nolan: *That's just the level of enthusiasm a guy hopes for when he makes a date with a pretty lady. Now what's your address?*

I practically flew through the next twenty-four hours, excited about my date with Agnes. I knew we'd be stuck sitting through a bunch of boring speeches, but after the speeches there would be dancing. I loved to dance. I was looking forward to holding Agnes in my arms and impressing her with my dance moves. And maybe, if I played my cards right, I could show her some other moves later.

Saturday night I pulled up to her house a few minutes before six. Agnes was standing on the porch waiting for me.

She was wearing a jade green dress that hugged her curves, ending with some kind of a flare a couple inches below her knees. She'd paired the dress with black patent leather shoes with chunky black heels. Her hair was pulled up into an up-do, several long tendrils loose and curling around her face. She didn't usually wear make-up, but tonight she'd done something to her eyes, making them look larger and mysterious.

I resisted the urge to suggest we go back into the house so I could ravage her.

"Well, aren't you looking beautiful tonight?"

Agnes's face flushed with pleasure. Her gaze traveled over the black suit I was wearing. It was tailored for me and fit perfectly. I pointed to my tie, which coincidentally was almost the same shade of green as her dress.

"We match. People will think we planned that."

She gave me a smile and headed towards my SUV. "Shall we?"

We talked easily on the way to the hotel where the event was being held. It was about thirty minutes away, but the drive passed quickly. I pulled up to the valet line, handed the keys to the attendant, then took her arm and led her towards the main entrance.

Flashbulbs went off as we walked up to the door. While I was a minor celebrity in this area, mostly from my years playing with Atlanta, I knew they were after more famous people than I was. Agnes flinched as the photographers got moved closer.

"Not a fan of photos?"

"I've always hated the paparazzi."

"Do you have a famous past I don't know about?" I asked, knowing that average people did not come into contact with paparazzi on a regular basis.

"I don't, but my daddy does."

Chapter Seven - Agnes

I could've bitten my own tongue off for sharing that little tidbit. I figured that there was no way that Nolan was going to let that one slide. Fortunately, he just gave me a curious look but didn't ask while we were around the reporters, which I appreciated. Not that they would easily connect me to Igor anyway, given our different last names.

We walked into the hotel, his hand on my elbow burning me like a brand. I couldn't decide how I felt about this date tonight. Liz had ambushed me at book club, talking Nolan up and encouraging me to give him a shot. All the ladies at our table, filled with romantic notions about how I must be the month's "love winner" based on the supposed parallels between the book and my connection to Nolan, joined in the cajoling me until I'd had no choice but to give in.

Although if I was being totally honest, I wasn't hating the idea. Ever since we'd shared that kiss in the storage room, I'd been fantasizing about doing it again. I'd gotten to know Nolan pretty well over the last month, and the more I got to know him, the more I liked him. I could maybe get past our age difference, but the athlete factor made me nervous. There was no way I wanted to end up like my mother, being made a fool of by an athlete.

"He's moving into team management when he retires at the end of the season," Liz had argued when I said I didn't date athletes. "He'll only be a professional athlete for a few more months."

Of course the other ladies at our table had agreed. Between them, they'd convinced me to give Nolan a shot.

Nolan and I entered the ballroom and quickly found our table. We were seated with Liz's parents, who owned the team, Liz, and several other senior staff and their dates. Liz was the only person there without a date, much to her mother's annoyance.

"I hate even numbers at a dinner," Mrs. McNally whispered loud enough for our half of the table to hear. "I just wish you'd find someone nice and settle down, Liz. Look at Nolan and Agnes here."

"Maybe I'll find a match at book club," Liz told her, sending me a wink. She appeared completely unconcerned about her mother's judgement, which I had to admire, given the glare her mother sent her.

"What kind of book club is this you're going to?" Nolan asked curiously.

"Never mind, it's just a ridiculous thing people believe based on coincidences."

"It doesn't sound like just coincidences to me," Liz replied. "Not after I heard firsthand about all the love connections."

Before anyone could ask more questions, we were interrupted by the arrival of the food. We ate a mediocre dinner and listened to several mediocre speeches before the program was finally over and the band came on. The minute they started playing music, Nolan smiled and grabbed my hand.

"Let's dance."

I'd always liked to dance, so I willingly followed him out on the floor. We danced two faster songs before the band played a slower tune. Nolan pulled me into his arms, and I relaxed against his chest, subtly inhaling the spicy scent of his cologne. I wasn't a small woman, but in Nolan's arms, I felt tiny. Protected. Comfortable.

We made our way through the two slow songs, wrapped in a sensual dance cocoon before the music picked up again. We stepped apart, and I wondered if I looked as dazed as I felt. Or maybe horny was a better word. My entire body was vibrating with awareness, and it took everything in me not to push Nolan to the floor and have my way with him right here in the ballroom. Based on the bulge pressing against my stomach, he felt the same.

I looked up to see Liz grinning at us from across the dance floor where she was dancing with her father. She sent me a thumbs up from behind his back, which I ignored.

"You ready to get out of here?" Nolan asked me, his gaze more serious than I'd ever seen it.

"Sure."

We walked hand in hand out of the ballroom and I found myself wishing that we had a room at the hotel. The drive back to my house was almost silent, both of us lost in our own thoughts. Mine were solely about how much I wanted Nolan and I was pretty sure his were too, because when we pulled into my driveway, he gave me a searching look.

"Can I come in?"

"I don't have any coffee," I teased.

He reached across the car, cupping my cheek with one large hand. I leaned into his touch.

"I'm not interested in coffee."

"Really? What are you interested in then?" I teased.

"You. I'd like to spend the night," he told me, and I felt a little shiver of excitement slide down my spine. "You can say no if you're not ready, but if you are, I'd really like to come in and finish what we started on the dance floor."

"I want you," I admitted. "But I'm not in a place where I want something serious."

I appreciated him not pointing out that only a week ago I'd told him I wasn't interested in a one-night stand. I was annoyed by my own flip flopping. The truth was, I didn't know what I wanted when it came to Nolan. Or maybe it was more accurate to say that I knew what I wanted, but I didn't trust that I could have it. I was giving him mixed signals and I knew it.

"I hear you, but I reserve the right to try to change your mind."

"I won't change my mind," I said, not sure which one of us I was trying to convince.

His look was full of an arrogance that made me want to smack him, or kiss him, I wasn't quite sure.

"We'll see how you feel when I've got my head between your thighs and you're screaming my name."

Moisture flooded my panties as I damn near came on the spot. I pulled away and opened the passenger door.

"Come on big talker," I teased, "Let's see what you got."

Nolan followed me to the porch of my little house, staying close enough behind me that I could feel the heat of his body warming up my back. I opened the door and as we entered the living room, I gestured with my hand.

"This is the living room. The kitchen is back there. Let's finish the tour upstairs."

He chuckled as I grabbed his hand and pulled him up the staircase behind me. "Nice place."

I suddenly wondered what his place looked like. Although I knew triple A baseball likely didn't pay a lot, I knew enough to know that the professional athletes made good money. If he'd spent ten years in the majors, he'd likely made more than enough money than he needed to be comfortable for the rest of his life.

Assuming he hadn't squandered it all, that is. My daddy had pissed away millions of dollars in his lifetime. The man couldn't hold onto a dollar if his life depended on it.

"Thanks. Where do you live?" I asked.

"I live on the bluff overlooking the beach. I bought the place with my signing bonus from Atlanta."

I realized that Nolan must live in the same neighborhood as Evie's friend Emma who was part of the book club. She'd married a billionaire who had a fancy place up there.

"Great, that's enough small talk. Let's get naked."

Chapter Eight - Nolan

I burst out laughing at Agnes' comment, then stopped laughing as she whipped her dress over her head, revealing a body that was soft and womanly. I pressed a hand against my cock to calm him down as I took in her black lace bra and matching panties.

"Wow."

She raised one eyebrow and I got to work removing my suit, picking up on her subtle hint.

"Boxer briefs, I knew it," she murmured, her eyes fixed on the bulge in my underwear.

"You thought about my underwear?"

Her eyes raised to mine. "Did I say that out loud?"

"Yep." I crooked my finger at her. "Come here."

She came closer, and I threaded my fingers through her hair and pressed my lips against hers. She opened with a sigh, and I sucked her tongue into my mouth, exploring it with my own. Agnes slid her hands down my sides to the waistband of my briefs, sliding them down my hips. Her hand closed around my cock, and I groaned against her mouth.

"We should slow down, or this will be over way faster than it should be."

"We don't need to focus on 'shoulds', we need to focus on what feels good," she said, giving my cock a little squeeze.

I groaned and backed Agnes up to the bed. When the back of her knees hit the bed, she sat down. I dropped to my knees, removing her shoes, then moved my hands to the waistband of her lacy black panties.

"What are you doing?"

"I believe I promised to make you scream my name, darlin'."

One hand came to my shoulder, stopping my movement. "Just so you know, I don't wax."

Her tone indicated that she thought that would be a problem for me.

"You don't need to wax for me."

I slid her panties down over her hips, tossing them behind me. My gaze dropped to her neatly trimmed pussy and my mouth watered at the sight of her. Before she could say anything, I grabbed her legs, tossing them over my shoulders, which forced her to lean back on her elbows. I lowered my head and gave her one long lick, making Agnes groan my name.

"Nolan!"

"Shh, just relax. I've got you."

Using my fingers to spread her lower lips, I began exploring her pussy with my tongue. She tasted sweet and a little bit tangy. Agnes' hands came to my head, directing me where she wanted me most, and I complied, focusing my attention just to the side of her clit.

She stared at the ceiling, biting her lip as if to keep quiet. That wouldn't do. I reached up and tugged her lip away gently.

"I want to hear you." Her head popped up, staring at me.

I slid one finger into her slick channel, pumping in and out, and sucked her little clit into my mouth. It didn't take long before Agnes was flying, her back arching off the bed, thighs squeezing my head. My name was a loud groan from her lips as she succumbed to her orgasm. I watched her from beneath my lashes, enjoying the sight of Agnes' orgasm more than anything I'd ever seen before in my life.

When her movements slowed, I removed my finger and sat back on my heels, watching her recover. She breathed heavily for a minute or two, before pushing herself back up to seated.

"How about you take off that bra?"

She looked down, as if surprised she was still wearing it, then reached behind her to remove the contraption and free her breasts. Her breasts were on the larger side, round and pale, with dark pink nipples. Agnes seemed to grow nervous as I stared at them like I'd never seen tits before.

"I don't have the perky breasts of a twenty year old," she said, her voice a little unsure.

I met her eyes. "Your tits are freaking perfect, just like the rest of you."

I couldn't help but feel angry at whatever man had made her feel insecure. My hands closed around her breasts, squeezing and plumping them, and she gave me a sweet smile.

"Someday I'm going to fuck these beauties, but right now I want your pussy too much."

A slight pinkness crept across her cheeks and I chuckled.

"You're not embarrassed about a little dirty talk, are you darlin'?"

Instead of answering, she leaned forward and kissed me long and hard. I took over, deepening the kiss even more as I continued to explore her beautiful breasts with my hands. When I couldn't take it anymore, I pulled away.

"I'm going to die if I don't get inside you now," I said fervently.

She scooted back. "There are condoms in the drawer."

I pushed down the ridiculous flash of jealousy about her having condoms here. Obviously Agnes had been with other men, like I'd been with other women. It didn't matter who came before me, because I knew in my heart she was the last woman I would ever sleep with. And I was going to do my best to ensure that I was the last man she ever even looked at.

After rolling on the condom, I crawled up the bed, doing a reverse push-up to lower myself over Agnes. Settling the weight of my lower body between her legs, I kissed her again. I couldn't get enough of kissing her, she was like a drug.

When I pulled back again, her eyes were bright with need. "Are you ready, Agnes?"

"Yes."

I slid into her slowly, giving her time to adjust, and when I bottomed out deep inside her, she brought her legs around my hips, hooking her feet at the small of my back. I started thrusting in and out of her, slowly at first, then picking up speed, as Agnes met me stroke for stroke. We matched each other's rhythm effortlessly, totally in sync.

"You feel so good," I gasped.

I recited my career statistics in my head, trying my best to distract myself long enough for Agnes to get her second orgasm. I slowed down our pace, deliberately sliding my pelvis against her clit with every pass, until she was shaking beneath me.

"I need you to come," I bit out. "I'm close."

Our eyes met and held as I once again picked up the pace. I felt almost frantic as I pounded into her, and maybe she liked it a little rougher too because it didn't take long before she was squeezing my dick and chanting my name over and over like a prayer.

That was all I needed to let go, pushing into her in several long strokes as I released my seed into the condom. I came so hard I could hear my blood rushing in my ears and when it was over, I was pretty sure I'd died and gone to heaven.

Chapter Nine - Agnes

I liked waking up in Nolan's arms more than I would ever admit. I tended to be cold in the morning, but he was like a giant furnace behind me. I sighed happily and bent my knees so I could rest the soles of my cold feet against his shins.

"Ah!" he yelped. "Your feet are like ice!"

I giggled. "Thanks for warming them up."

"I'll warm you up all right."

The poke of something hard against my backside gave me a hint of what was to come. He slid his leg between mine, raising my top leg and running his already-hard cock down my ass crack and in between my lower lips.

"Mmm." I moaned happily as I felt him press against my entrance, then stiffened. "Oh wait, we need a condom."

I was tempted to tell him we could skip it, and that freaked me the hell out. I reached forward, grabbing one from the table, then handing it back to him. I heard him behind me, sheathing himself up before he lifted my leg again and slid between my folds. One arm stretched over me to cup my breast, while the other slid underneath my neck like a pillow. I reached up to lace my fingers through his and sighed as Nolan eased himself inside me.

"Agnes," he growled, his voice rough with sleep. "You feel so good."

Nolan peppered my shoulder and neck with little kisses as he made love to me slowly from behind, his movements leisurely. The hand on my breast slid slowly down my body, circling my belly button before moving over my mound to find my clit.

"Nolan." I gasped his name as his fingers tapped against the bundle of nerves.

My orgasm was almost gentle, moving through me in slow waves instead of violently crashing through me like it had last night, but it was perfect for my half-awake state. My toes curled, my back arched, and I threw my head back onto Nolan's shoulder, sighing happily as I reached my completion.

It only took a few more gentle strokes before Nolan groaned my name, and I felt the warmth of his seed through the latex barrier inside me. When it was over he pulled me closer, wrapping himself around me from behind, our bodies still attached. Eventually he stirred.

"I should deal with the condom."

I snuggled into the blankets while he went to the bathroom, returning a few moments later. He sat on the bed, leaning down to kiss my forehead.

"I have to go to a team meeting later today, but could I buy you breakfast first?"

My first instinct was to say no. I'd said I wanted casual. I'd said I didn't want a relationship with him. But I couldn't deny the desire to spend more time with him, no matter what my intentions had been last night.

"Breakfast sounds good."

I saw him release a breath. "Great, how about the diner? I could go for some waffles."

"Love it. Let me brush my teeth and get dressed."

A little while later we were seated at a booth in the diner downtown, tucking into huge breakfast platters. We'd both worked up an appetite since dinner last night.

"Hey Agnes."

I looked up and suppressed a groan as I saw Evie striding towards my table, her boyfriend the sheriff right behind her. The peril of living in a small town was that you rarely did anything in public without running into someone you knew. I liked Evie, but I knew she also tended to be a bit of a gossip.

"Hey Evie. Hi Jake. How are you?"

Evie reached down to give me a hug, then gave Nolan a sharp look. "Let me guess, you're the baseball player?"

"Are you a fan?" Nolan asked politely, giving her what I thought of as his 'public persona smile'.

"Nope, not a fan, not at all."

Nolan shot me a look of confusion. Meanwhile, Evie reached back and slapped the back of her hand on the sheriff's abdomen.

"See? I told you the book club had another love connection."

He gave her a long-suffering look. "Yes, you did."

He reached a hand out to Nolan. "I don't think we've met. I'm Sheriff Jake Wilson."

Nolan shook his hand. "Nolan Jacobs."

"You play for the Seagulls right?"

"Yeah, I'm the starting pitcher."

"It's funny, we were just reading a book about a baseball player in our book club last month," Evie said. "It was a romance book with an age gap. Kind of an opposites attract kind of thing. It's about a baseball player at the end of his career who falls in love."

Nolan nodded politely, obviously unsure what was happening. He glanced at me.

"Evie runs a book club out of her store, Boozy Books," I explained. "Some women in the book club have fallen in love with characters similar to books we've read, so now she thinks because we read a book about a baseball player and you happen to be a ball player, that must mean we'll fall in love."

Nolan shot Evie a curious look. "Has this happened a lot?"

"Yep. We read a book about a billionaire, and my friend fell in love with one. We read a book about a firefighter, and my other friend fell in love with the fire chief. We read a..."

She stopped as Jake elbowed her and grumbled. "He gets the idea."

"Are you shushing me?"

The gaze she turned on to her boyfriend was lethal. He held up his hands in supplication.

"Of course not, honey. I wouldn't dare."

She narrowed her eyes at him, and he glared right back. These two were oil and water, each giving as good as they got, but underneath all their bickering was a strong love that was obvious to everyone who spent time with them. I cleared my throat.

"Well, thanks for stopping by to say hi. It was nice seeing you two."

They took the hint and left me alone with Nolan, heading out of the restaurant.

"Is this the same book club that you brought Liz to?" he asked.

"Yeah."

"What's the next book you're reading after the baseball one?"

"Something about a chef," I said. "I don't remember the details."

"Well, that's good news. Liz is a terrible cook. She set her kitchen on fire once. She needs a personal chef in her life."

My mouth dropped. "You think Liz is going to fall in love with a chef now?"

"Sounds like it's fated to happen for someone, why not Liz?"

When I continued to stare at him he added, "I'm a baseball player. We're very superstitious. Deal with it."

Chapter Ten - Nolan

"How's it going with you and Agnes?"

I couldn't help but smile as Liz approached me while I recovered in an ice bath a couple of weeks later after a hard game.

Her eyes fell to my shoulder. "And how's your shoulder feeling?"

"Both things are going great."

When I didn't say anything, she tapped her foot impatiently. "I helped you get Agnes to that boring ass event, and I have no life of my own. The least you can do is dish a little."

"You're right," I acknowledged. "We've been dating since the event and spending a lot of time together when we're not on the road for away games."

"Well, that sounds promising."

Liz must have seen something on my face because she sat on a nearby bench and asked, "What?"

"When we're together everything's great, but when we're not, sometimes she gets kind of distant. It's like she starts to talk herself out of being with me," I explained. "Also, she's holding herself back. Whenever I ask her about it, she keeps bringing up our age difference or the fact that I'm a professional athlete."

"A woman gets to a certain point in her life, and she's got a lot of baggage from past relationships," Agnes said philosophically. "Add to that a society that discounts women over thirty, and a father that was a rat bastard man whore, and I'm not surprised she's leery of a relationship."

Liz's word reminded me of the comment Agnes had made when we ran into the paparazzi at the press event. She'd said that her father was famous, but then we'd gotten distracted, and I never asked what she meant.

"Her father?" I asked, not feeling the slightest bit guilty about pumping Liz for information about my girlfriend.

"You don't know who her father is?" Liz asked incredulously.

"I wouldn't be asking if I did," I snapped. "She's never said a word about him."

"Her father is Igor Scottchevsky, the hockey player."

"Scottchevsky?" I asked.

"I guess her mother shortened their name to Scott after she and Igor got divorced, as a way to distance the family from his antics."

I'd never paid much attention to sports that weren't baseball, but even I had heard of Igor Scottchevsky. He was the type of guy the paparazzi loved, always engaged in crazy antics like ice skating naked at Rockefeller Plaza or getting arrested for drunk driving. And always, always with a young, busty puck bunny on his arm. I had no idea that Igor had been married with a wife and kids. Suddenly Agnes' loathing of athletes and photographers was making a bit more sense.

To my surprise, the woman in question walked into the treatment room. Agnes had spent so much time at the stadium that all the security personnel knew her now and let her have free rein. As we spent more time together, she'd started attending the occasional game, which made me ridiculously happy.

"Nice game," Agnes said, her eyes drifting downward to the outline of my cock beneath the ice water before snapping back up. Her cheeks turned a bit pink, and I wondered if she knew about what cold water did to a guy's junk.

"We lost," I reminded her.

"But you tried your best, right?"

I smirked. "You know this wasn't a Little League game, right babe?"

Her eyes snagged mine at the endearment, but she didn't comment. Instead, she turned to greet Liz.

"Hey Liz, how's everything?"

"Pretty good. I was reading our book club book and hoping to meet a chef to fall in love with, but I guess someone else is getting lucky this month."

"Oh my God, not you too Liz," Agnes groaned. "I swear this Boozy Book Club love connection talk is getting totally out of hand. A bunch of grown women acting like lovestruck teenagers, it's crazy."

"Well, you can't argue with the results," Liz said, looking between us with a raised eyebrow.

"What are you doing now?" I asked Agnes, interrupting before she burst poor Liz's bubble.

I hoped my friend would find someone of her own; she was awesome.

"Actually, I was wondering if you'd like to come over for dinner." She winked at Liz. "I didn't fall in love with a chef or anything, but I think I can manage to cook something edible."

The moment felt significant. Usually, I made the first move with Agnes, suggesting getting together. Her asking me first felt like progress.

"I'd love to," I said, rising from the ice bath. "Just let me take a quick shower."

It didn't escape me that Agnes moved in front of Liz, as if to block her view of my naked body. There was no such thing as modesty in the locker room, but this little display of jealousy felt like more progress. Maybe things were going to turn around with my Agnes after all.

***

"Tell me about your family," I asked later that night.

Agnes stiffened in my arms for a split second. "My family? Why do you ask?"

After a delicious dinner of grilled chicken, mashed potatoes, green beans and salad, Agnes and I had snuggled on the couch watching a movie. When the movie finished, we'd headed upstairs, and she'd ridden me like a horse until I thought I was going to pass out from pleasure.

The more time we spent in the bedroom, the more uninhibited she became. I wasn't sure if it was because she was more confident that my attraction for her was real, or just her becoming more comfortable with me. Possibly a bit of both. Whatever the reason, she was as insatiable as I was. We couldn't seem to get enough of each other.

"It's a natural thing to talk about your family when you're dating a person. I've told you all about my parents, but you haven't really mentioned your family at all."

"Um. Well. I was born and raised in Mobile, Alabama," she started, speaking slowly. "My mama was a single mother for most of my childhood. She and Daddy got divorced when my youngest sister was a toddler, and we didn't see too much of him after that."

"So, you have siblings?" I asked, sidestepping the father question.

"Yeah, I have two sisters, one older, one younger. One lives up in Chicago, and the other still lives in Alabama."

"Are you close with them?" I asked.

"I don't know that I'd say we are close. My two sisters are pretty tight with each other. Honestly, I always felt like a bit of an outsider with them, but we've all been talking more lately, ever since my mama died."

I wrapped my arms around her, and Agnes snuggled into my chest, her cheek resting on my right pec. "I'm sorry about your mama."

"Thanks. She died rather suddenly a few months ago, but at least she went fast."

The silence stretched for a few minutes before I asked, "What about your father? Are you close?"

"Not at all," she said emphatically. "I haven't seen him in years. Sometimes I'll hear from him on my birthday, or one of my sisters' birthdays."

"Huh?"

"He'll usually remember that it's somebody's birthday, but not whose, so he'll call each of us until he hits the right daughter. Sometimes we mess with him and each of us pretends it's the other's birthday."

Her voice was casual, but there was an undercurrent of pain there. "The man doesn't have the calendar app on his phone?"

She burst out laughing. "Igor doesn't have time for such mundane things like calendars. Unless of course it's about hockey."

"Your father plays hockey?" I asked innocently.

"My father is Igor Scottchevsky. He was a player with Minnesota for many years, then he started coaching after he retired. I think he's a sports announcer or something now, I'm not really sure."

Her voice turned harder, signaling to me that it was time to change the subject.

"Speaking of sports, how about you come with me to an away game? The team is going to New York City and I'd love for you to come. We could play tourist."

Chapter Eleven - Agnes

"How's it going with Nolan?" my friend Tara asked the next night as we walked to happy hour.

We'd decided to join a few other book club members at Jose's, a Mexican restaurant in town that was known for its strong margaritas. It was a favorite hangout of Evie and her two besties, Dawn and Emma, and sometimes they extended an invitation to some of the other women from the book club to join them.

"It's going okay," I said.

"Just okay?"

"Well, good actually, really good." I couldn't help but smile. "We've been spending a lot of time together, and now he wants me to go to an away game with him so we can do a weekend in New York City."

"That sounds like fun."

It did. Most of the time I was really happy with Nolan, but sometimes the doubts crept in, and I worried we were getting too serious. He seemed like a wonderful guy, but what if I was missing some big character flaw? My gut said he was trust-worthy, but my mama had trusted Igor once too.

Tara's and my conversation stalled as we walked into the restaurant. Evie and her two best friends were there already when we walked in, along with Maisie, the assistant manager of Boozy Books. She was an old college friend of Evie's who'd moved to town a few months ago after a bad divorce – and her ex-husband's arrest for fraud.

"Hey ladies," Tara greeted the group as we reached the table. "Dawn, how's the baby?"

Dawn had gotten the surprise of her life last year when she'd gotten pregnant while she thought she was already in menopause. The father of the baby was her estranged ex-husband, who'd just come back to town to try to win her back. Now the two had an adorable baby girl, in addition to Chloe, the grown-up daughter they had from when they were teenagers.

"She's good, over there with her daddy and the guys."

Dawn pointed to a table where her ex-husband and now-fiancé Griffin sat with baby Ava strapped to his chest. Evie's boyfriend Jake, Emma's husband Wyatt, and Maisie's boyfriend Thom were also at the table. They were all surprisingly good looking. It was like a model call for a silver fox calendar over there.

"Yeah, the guys like to think they have to babysit us when we come here," Evie groused. "They still haven't gotten over that one time we got drunk and tried to capture the guy who was breaking into my bookstore. Even though we were successful, I might add."

Everyone in town had heard the story of how Evie and her friends had caught a criminal and solved a mystery using tricks right out of a Scooby Doo cartoon. Her boyfriend hadn't appreciated her taking the law into her hands, but my friends were quite proud of themselves.

"I wasn't involved in that little escapade of yours," Maisie protested. "I wasn't even living here in town then."

"Yeah but you get into enough trouble on your own," Evie teased. "Thom is probably afraid you're going to try to parallel park again if he doesn't keep an eye on you."

"Ha ha." Maisie rolled her eyes.

I poured myself a margarita and leaned back to enjoy the happy hour with my book club friends. I was glad I'd found this group of women, all strong and smart and interesting in their own way. Other than their obsession with book club matchups and love, I really liked spending time with them. Speaking of which...

"How's it going with your sexy baseball player?" Evie asked curiously. Everyone turned to look at me. "Y'all looked super cozy at breakfast a couple of weeks ago."

"He wants her to go to New York City with him for an away game," Tara interjected before I could open my mouth. "Then have a romantic weekend together in the city."

The women oohed like it was super significant.

"It doesn't mean anything. We're just having fun."

"Yeah, that's what I thought too," Dawn said wryly. "Until I wound up pregnant again."

"We always use condoms," I assured her.

"The point isn't that Dawn managed to bypass both a vasectomy and the onset of menopause to get knocked up," Evie told me. "The point is that she was deluding herself that it was just about having fun when everyone knew she was falling back in love with Griffin."

"I can keep my emotions separate from the physical side of things," I assured her, even as I knew I was lying. I was already in so deep with Nolan I wasn't sure how I'd survive if things went wrong.

Tara pinned me with a look. "Sure you can."

Tara's words were ringing in my ears when I went from happy hour right over to Nolan's house. As soon as he opened the door, he pulled me close, giving me a big hug. Nolan was a very affectionate guy, always hugging me or rubbing my shoulder or resting his hand on my leg. I'd never been one to crave affectionate touch, but with Nolan it felt natural.

"How was happy hour?" he asked.

"It was fun, but the girls were annoyed that their guys were at another table keeping an eye on them."

"Why would they do that?"

"Let me tell you some stories."

***

Two weeks later I was on a plane with Nolan. Since I was accompanying him, he was traveling separate from the team, although we'd meet up with them at the hotel. Nolan had a game tomorrow, then we'd added two more days to the trip so we could explore New York City over the weekend and see some of the sights. I'd never been to New York and found myself more excited than I'd expected. We'd spent hours debating what activities to do on our two free days in the city.

When we got to the hotel Nolan and I joined the team for dinner. It wasn't as common for wives and girlfriends to travel with their Triple A players, given that the budgets and salary scales were significantly lower than the major leagues, but there were still several other women there, as well as Liz. After spending so much time with the team working on the publicity campaign, I felt completely comfortable with the group.

I enjoyed dinner, joining in as the guys teased each other and gossiped like old ladies. It was nice how close this team was. They all seemed to get along well.

After dinner we headed up to our hotel room where Nolan and I relaxed in bed, reading. That was one thing I'd never expected from an athlete: a love of reading that rivaled my own. It turned out that Nolan was a voracious reader who read a little bit of everything. He was even reading "Extra Innings", the baseball book we'd read for book club.

"This book isn't like us at all," he said as he finished reading and set the book on the bedside table. "Other than an age difference and his career being baseball, there are no similarities to us at all."

"Right? I told the girls that, but they're all obsessed with making everyone's dating life connect to whatever we're reading."

Nolan rolled to his side, propping his head up on one hand, and gave me a smirk.

"Well, there's one other parallel between the book and us."

"What?"

"Hot sex."

Chapter Twelve - Nolan

As I ran out to the pitcher's mound for the first inning, my eyes sought out Agnes in the crowd. I'd pulled some strings to get her a seat in the first row, right behind the visiting team's dugout. I spotted her right away, wearing the Gulls jersey and hat I'd given her. She looked adorable wearing my number. I waved, pleased that she waved back despite the people looking at her.

Agnes had been to quite a few games now, and I found that I loved having her in the stands rooting for me. I'd always thought it was ridiculous when other guys used to insist on their wives and partners attending as many games as possible, but now I understood.

My girl still wasn't a huge fan of baseball, but she'd learned a bit about the game hanging out with me. She still pretended to hate sports, but I suspected that my love of baseball had rubbed off on her, at least a little bit.

The Seagulls played a good game, easily beating the New York team despite the high energy of the home crowd. I couldn't skip my physio appointments – otherwise I wouldn't be able to move my throwing arm tomorrow – but as soon as they were done massaging and icing my shoulder I hurried through my shower and put on my street clothes. I was eager to get back to Agnes so we could start our sightseeing weekend.

The tunnel outside the visitor's locker room was full of cleat chasers, the mostly young women who were looking to score with baseball players. Triple A teams like the Seagulls weren't as popular as the MLB players of course, but every cleat chaser dreamed of landing a young player who was on his way up to the majors.

One woman grabbed my arm as soon as I exited the locker room.

"Hey there handsome, you're the pitcher, right?"

I looked her up and down, noting the teased hair, heavy make-up, and the skin-tight baseball jersey that had been modified to highlight her impressive – and probably fake – cleavage. She'd tied the jersey at the waist, showing off her toned abs and revealing a micro skirt that was so short it was almost indecent.

When I'd been a young player, I'd partaken in plenty of what this woman was offering, but at this stage of my life, it just made me sad to see someone who thought they needed to snag an athlete to make them feel like they had value.

I paused, trying to extricate myself from the cleat chaser's talon-like fingers, and gave her a neutral smile, knowing that someone was always taking a picture or recording the players these days.

"Yes, I'm the pitcher. Did you want an autograph?"

"How about you buy me a drink instead?" she purred, pointing her breasts at me, and fluttering her fake eyelashes.

I subtly tried to tug my arm away from her again, but she held on tight, not getting the hint.

"How about you get your fake nails out of my boyfriend's arm?" Agnes' voice was colder than I'd ever heard it. "And have some self-respect while you're at it."

"Sorry, my girlfriend's here now." I turned and gave Agnes a smile. "Hi, darlin.'"

She smiled back, her expression turning warm. "Hi yourself. You ready to get out of here and start our weekend of fun?"

"Yes ma'am."

We left the cleat chaser to find her next victim and strolled arm in arm out of the stadium.

"You called me your boyfriend," I pointed out, feeling incredibly pleased about it. Agnes had never said that before, and I knew I was wearing a big, dopey smile.

"I did call you my boyfriend," she said. "But don't make me sorry I did by making a big deal out of it."

Her voice was teasing. That's one of the things I loved about Agnes, she was always giving me a hard time, but there was never any malice in it. She just had a teasing personality and a dry sense of humor.

"Okay, but I reserve the right to call you my girlfriend whenever I want now, *girlfriend*."

She gave me an aggrieved sigh. "I should have left you to baseball barbie."

I pulled her under my arm and tugged her into my side. "I'm glad you didn't. I've got something much better right here."

She wrapped her arm around my waist, settling in next to me. "Keep sweet talking, mister, and you'll get lucky later."

"I'm already lucky, babe."

Our two days in New York City flew by. We visited the Statue of Liberty, rode the carousel in Central Park, looked at the view from the Empire State Building, checked out some exhibits at the Museum of Modern Art, and even went to a Broadway play.

I was surprised how easily Agnes and I traveled together. We had a lot of similar interests, and neither of us were particularly rigid in our plans, allowing us to explore other things that caught our interest as we made our way through the day.

Things were going great until our last night in the city. We'd decided to splurge and get a fancy dinner, making reservations at a nice place a few blocks away from Times Square. I'd put on a suit and tie, and Agnes looked delectable in a form-fitting black dress and matching pumps. She'd pulled her hair up into a fancy up-do, and put on some eye make-up and lipstick.

We enjoyed a delicious dinner of steak and pasta and shared a bottle of wine. We were debating stopping some place for cheesecake on the way back to the hotel when we heard an accented voice bellow out nearby.

"Agnes? Is that you, girl?"

Agnes stiffened, the color draining from her face. Her father stood a few feet away, his arm around a young woman who couldn't have been more than twenty-two. Igor Scottchevsky was a big, burly guy, but he'd gone soft since he'd stopped playing hockey, getting a little thick around the middle. He was still handsome, with thick black hair shot through with silver, and a closely cropped beard. No doubt the cameras loved him.

"Hi Igor." My girlfriend's voice was lacking in enthusiasm.

"Aren't you going to give your old man a hug?" Igor bellowed as several heads turned our way.

I saw Agnes debate whether to give the man a hug or risk making more of a scene, then decide to take the easier option. She stood up, standing stiffly as her father pulled her into a hug that looked more performative than affectionate.

"What are you doing in New York, Igor?" she asked as she pulled away. "You're a long way from Minnesota, and hockey season is over."

"I had an important meeting at International Sports Network," he said loudly, puffing up his chest proudly. "I'm sure you've seen me on that program Hockey Center."

I vaguely remembered hearing that he had moved from coaching to being a hockey announcer on the sports network. The young woman with Igor cleared her throat, drawing the older man's attention.

"Elena, this is my middle daughter Agnes. Agnes, my girlfriend Elena."

"Nice to meet you," Agnes murmured, her voice brittle.

"Pleased to meet you," Elena said in a breathy, high pitched voice that made Agnes wince.

I touched Agnes' elbow, silently offering support, and she startled, like she hadn't remembered I was still there with her. The other two looked at Agnes expectantly.

"Igor, Elena," she started, her tone grudging. "This is my boyfriend Nolan."

"Nice to meet you both," I said politely, holding my hand out to her father.

Igor gripped my hand in a bruising grip, trying to show his dominance. I let him have the win, I didn't need to injure my pitching hand just to prove a point to this asshole.

"What do you do, son?"

I glanced at Agnes out of the corner of my eye. She was still as a statue, staring at the floor.

"I'm a baseball player."

"You with the Yankees then?"

"No, the Bay City Seagulls. Triple A."

"What's the matter Agnes," Igor boomed, derision on his face, "You couldn't get yourself a major league boyfriend?"

Agnes' face flushed with anger. She grabbed my hand and pulled me away from him, and I couldn't help but appreciate her mama bear routine.

"We need to go," she said, grabbing the check off the table and moving towards the door. "Bye Igor. Elena."

"Tell your mama I said hello. She must be proud you also hooked yourself an athlete, even if he is only a minor league player."

Agnes spun around angrily. "She's dead, asshole."

"What?" The cocky demeanor faltered. "Your mama passed? When did that happen?"

"Right after Christmas. Margaret notified your agent, but we never heard a word from you."

"He never told me the news." For a moment, Igor looked sad. "I'm sorry to hear that, Agnes, your mama was a great gal."

If looks could kill, Igor would be dead right in the middle of one of Manhattan's fanciest restaurants. Agnes stood there, vibrating with anger, while the diners around us watched us like we were dinner theater. I tugged on her hand.

"Come on babe. Let's get out of here."

Chapter Thirteen - Agnes

Nolan and I walked back to our hotel in silence, his fingers wrapped around mine, keeping me grounded. My head was swirling with emotions. Anger at my father. Sadness for my mama. Embarrassment that my father – or anyone – thought I might be with Nolan just because he was an athlete. Most of all, I was feeling disappointment. Our perfect vacation had been ruined with one Igor drive-by.

I hadn't seen the man in at least five years, maybe longer. It figured that we'd be in one of the largest cities in the world and manage to run into each other. When he'd talked about my mama, it had taken every ounce of self-control to keep myself from strangling him.

When we got back to the hotel, Nolan asked, "What do you need, babe?"

He seemed so good. But was he too good to be true? I was so confused.

He's not your daddy, I reminded myself. *Igor isn't half the man Nolan is.*

"I need to talk to my sisters."

We weren't super close, but we always had each other's back. I never doubted that they'd be there if I needed them, the same way I would do for them. They were the only two people on Earth who could understand exactly how I felt after running into our father and his latest barely-legal girlfriend.

Nolan nodded. "I can take a walk and give you some privacy."

I put my hand on his arm. "No, you don't need to leave, I was just going to text with them anyway."

Neither of my sisters liked talking on the phone. I updated my sisters on what happened via text while Nolan got ready for bed. He settled on the other end of the loveseat from me to read, his presence steady and supportive. After my sisters and I chatted about what an asshole our father was and how he was dating yet another girl who was younger than us, I felt a little calmer. The conversation then turned to Nolan.

Margaret: *What's the story with you and the ball player?*

Agnes: *Nolan? I met him because I'm doing PR for his team.*

Barbara: *Is it serious? Traveling together sounds serious.*

Agnes: *Kind of? But I think I should break up with him.*

Margaret: *Why?*

Agnes: *We all promised each other we'd never date an athlete.*

Margaret: *We were teenagers then. Not every athlete is going to be an asshole like Igor. The important thing isn't his profession, it's how he treats you.*

Barbara: *Exactly. Does he get drunk and throw things at you while screaming insults?*

Agnes: *No, he doesn't drink during the season other than the occasional beer or glass of wine.*

Margaret: *Is he selfish? Cold? Neglectful?*

Agnes: *No, he's the most attentive, affectionate, and considerate man I've dated.*

Barbara: *Does he flirt with the baseball equivalent of puck bunnies and pretend like he has no control over their actions?*

Agnes: *No, I saw him earlier this week with a cleat chaser and he was trying hard to disengage from her, without even knowing I was around. In fact, he looked disgusted by her.*

Barbara: *Is he sexist? Homophobic?*

Agnes: *No.*

Barbara: *Then he sounds nothing like Igor. Nothing at all.*

Margaret: *Okay, now that we've established he's nothing like our daddy, it's time for the million dollar question. How is he in bed?*

Agnes: *That's personal.*

Margaret: *Okay, he's a total stud in the sack. Good for you, sis.*

Agnes: *I didn't say that.*

Margaret: *If he was bad in bed, you'd say that he was bad, so you saying it's personal tells me he's good in bed. Am I wrong?*

Agnes: *No, you're not wrong.*

Margaret: *Sounds like your guy is a keeper, sis. Good men don't come around too often.*

Barbara: *Margaret's right. Quit talking to us, stop worrying about turning into Mama, and go get yourself some good loving from your hunky baseball man.*

After signing off with my sisters, I got ready for bed. Heading for the king sized bed, I settled underneath the covers. Nolan got into the other side, opening his arm across the bed. I took the invitation and slid over to rest my head on his bare chest, my arm flung across his stomach. He wrapped his arm around my shoulders. I inhaled his comforting scent.

He didn't ask me to talk, and somehow that made me want to talk, even though I didn't think I would.

"Do you know about my father?" I asked.

"Some. I don't really follow hockey but he's, um, been in the tabloids a lot so..."

"Yeah. He was a philandering asshole. Always getting into fights with people and having embarrassing drunken incidents. He publicly cheated on my mother, then punished her for asking for a divorce by suing her for custody and using us as pawns."

I took a breath.

"He was totally irresponsible, always 'forgetting' to send child support even though he was making a small fortune and we were barely getting by on my mama's salary. He'd promise to come visit, then not show up. Things like that. Thank God we had our mama, because that man was totally useless."

"That sucks, Agnes. I'm so sorry that happened."

Something inside me relaxed. I didn't talk about my father that often, but when I did, people would usually do one of two things: try to justify his bad behavior and assure me that he must love me "in his own way" or tell me it wasn't really as bad as I thought it was. Nolan accepting what I told him and not arguing about it meant the world to me.

I scooted up and laid myself on top of him, balancing with my hands on the mattress just above his shoulders. I looked down at him, searching his eyes in the dim light.

"Thanks for understanding," I whispered.

I lowered my head and kissed him deeply, sweeping my tongue into his mouth, tangling my fingers in his hair. Nolan let me take the lead. I kissed him until I ran out of breath, then kissed my way down his chest to his abdomen. Sliding his boxers down his thighs, I freed his cock. He was already hard as a rock.

I loved this feeling. I loved knowing that I had this effect on him. I loved how easy our relationship was. And for the first time ever, I admitted to myself that I loved him. I wasn't ready to say it yet, but I set out to show him.

I kissed the head of his cock, then teased the tip of my tongue around the mushroom head. Nolan groaned as I took him deeper, bringing him to the back of my throat. His fingers came to my hair.

"Agnes."

I hummed in response, and his eyes closed tightly. Moving my head up and down, I added suction, sliding my tongue along the underside of his cock with every upward stroke. Feeling his body tightening, I reached between his legs with one hand, cupping his balls and giving them a gentle squeeze. My other hand slid beneath his muscled ass, finding his back opening, and sliding one finger in slowly. His hips popped up, making his cock bounce against the back of my throat.

I continued to tease him with my hands and mouth until he bit out, "Agnes, I'm going to come."

This time I lightly dragged my teeth along his length, and that was all it took for him to release his seed into my mouth with a long groan. I drank it all down, and when he finally sagged back to the mattress, I slid back up his body and set my head against his chest again.

"When I can move again, I'll return the favor and make you feel good," he promised.

I lifted my head and met his eyes. "You already did."

I fell asleep nestled in the crook of his arm.

Chapter Fourteen - Nolan

I stared up at the ceiling, listening to the even sounds of Agnes sleeping. I'd been scared to death she was going to break up with me when we got back to the hotel. In the moment her father had appeared and disparaged us both, I could see all her doubts come rushing back.

She'd seemed better after she'd texted with her sisters for a while. When she'd confided in me about her father, I'd braced myself for what would happen next. But Agnes had surprised me – and not just by giving me a blow job. It meant the world to me that she hadn't lumped in with that jackass who'd fathered her.

One thing I knew for sure: I was completely in love with her. I had been since the moment I'd set eyes on her, and my love had only strengthened since then. We'd been together for a couple of months now, and I was ready to take things to the next level. I just wasn't sure if Agnes was ready.

I decided to play it cool for a while. As the next few weeks passed, it was clear that things had changed between us while we'd been in New York City. Agnes was more open with her affections now, and every time she introduced me as her boyfriend, I wanted to burst with pride.

A few weeks later, I was playing a weekday game when I had a little accident that once again changed the course of our relationship. It was a warm day in late Spring, and the Gulls were playing a team from Texas. Midway through the fifth inning, a player from Texas hit a line drive that glanced right off my head.

Everything slowed down for a moment. My hat flew off. I heard the gasp of the crowd. I felt the impact of the ball ringing through my head. I staggered for a moment, then dropped to my knees. Within seconds the medical team was on the field, assessing me.

"I'm fine," I said, "It didn't hit me directly."

"You're already getting a bump," the team doc said sternly. "You know the concussion protocol. You're going to the ER."

"Fine, but let me leave the field under my own power."

He helped me to my feet, releasing me to walk on my own. The crowd rose to their feet, cheering, and I waved, then immediately regretted it. Damn it, my head really hurt. As the doc walked me past the dugout, I caught my coach's eye.

"Have Liz call Agnes."

"You got it."

Forty-five minutes later I was on a gurney in the ER, hooked up to monitors, when I heard a commotion outside.

"Ma'am! Ma'am! You can't go back there."

"Nolan?"

I smiled as I heard Agnes' voice. The trainer who'd accompanied me to the hospital pulled the curtain back. "He's in here, Agnes."

My girlfriend rushed in looking frantic.

"Oh my God Nolan, are you okay?"

She grabbed my hand, her eyes bouncing around to look at the monitors, the IV in my hand, and finally the bandage wrapped around my head. Her eyes looked huge in her pale face.

"I'll be fine," I reassured her.

"Liz said you got hit in the head with a ball. I was scared to death."

"It was just a fluke accident. There's less than a one percent chance that a pitcher will be hit by a ball, but after playing all these years, I guess it was bound to happen eventually."

She blinked away tears, and I squeezed her hand. "Don't worry, I have a very hard head."

The trainer cleared his throat. "I'm going to get back to the stadium unless you need me, Nolan?"

"Thanks, I'm good. I got my girl here now."

We were silent until the trainer left, then Agnes met my eyes.

"Are you really okay?"

"Slight concussion, nothing serious, I promise."

She stared at me for a long moment, then shook her head.

"You don't know how to duck? I'd think they would teach you in Little League."

I burst out laughing, then grabbed my head as a stabbing pain hit me.

"Don't make me laugh, at least not until the pain meds kick in."

"Okay, but I'm going to yell at you about this later. The last thing I wanted to happen was to get a call that the man I love was going to the emergency room."

Everything inside me stilled. "You love me?"

Our eyes met. "Yeah," she said softly. "I do."

"That's good, because I love you too. And it's not just the head injury talking."

I tugged on her hand, and she moved forward to meet me in a quick kiss. When she pulled away, Agnes cupped my cheek in one hand.

"I'm going to stay with you until you've recovered from your concussion."

"I hope you'll stay with me forever, love."

Epilogue - Agnes

"And playing the last game of his career, give a big Seagulls welcome to our pitcher, Nolan Jacobs."

The crowd roared as Nolan jogged out onto the field, waving his hat in greeting. After his two stints with the team, he was one of their most beloved players. Last night there had been a large public event for fans to say goodbye, and now the stands were packed with people ready to watch him pitch his final game.

I was in the front row right behind the home team dugout, wearing Nolan's jersey. I had my friend Tara on one side of me, and Nolan's mother on the other side. I'd met Nolan's family when he was recovering from his concussion, and since then I'd seen them several times. He had a great family and I got along well with them.

After this last game, Nolan was going to take a couple of weeks off before starting his new job in management on November first. We'd already planned a weeklong vacation in Belize for his time off.

The Gulls were playing a great game, and when it was time for the Seventh Inning Stretch, to my surprise Nolan was giving the microphone instead of the announcer who normally led the fans through the traditional song.

He stood on the field, turning in a circle while he sang, waving his arms to ramp up the fans. When he finished the iconic song, he offered a few words of gratitude to all the people who'd supported him in his career, including his famous godfather who he had been named for.

"Before the Seagulls finish winning this game...," he paused while the crowd cheered and the visiting team booed. "I'd like to do one more thing."

He strode over to where I was sitting, passing the dugout on his way, eyes fixed on me the whole time. His coach handed him something, then Nolan stopped in front of me and dropped to one knee on the grass.

"Agnes, for as long as I can remember, baseball was my life. And then I met you, and you became my life too." He paused again as every woman in the place reacted with a sigh. "Please, will you marry me?"

I stared at him for a long moment until Tara poked me in the ribs. I moved closer to the short wall that separated the spectators from the field.

"Yes Nolan, I will marry you."

Nolan leapt to his feet, reaching up and grabbing my waist to drag me over the wall while the crowd began clapping and cheering.

He slipped the engagement ring onto my finger, a beautiful ruby surrounded by tiny diamonds, then pulled me into his arms for a long, deep kiss. When we finally pulled apart, he gave me a tender smile.

"You've made me very happy Agnes. I'll thank you properly after the game."

"You'd better."

***

Be sure to check out the rest of the Boozy Book Club series, including Evie's story, "Martinis & Mysteries[1]", available everywhere now.

If you liked this book, please show me some love, and leave a review. Good reviews are like puppies, they make everyone feel happy.

Keep reading for a special excerpt from "Summer Wedding[2]," available now.

---

1. https://books2read.com/u/31e7Mr

2.   https://books2read.com/u/bOzQ5g

Special Preview

Summer Wedding by Rose Bak

"Uncle Reed, when will you get here?"

I smiled at Jonathon's eager tone, even though he couldn't exactly see me through the car dashboard.

"I'm pulling into the parking lot now," I told him as I swung into an open parking spot that came up unexpectedly. "I'll...oh shit!"

"What's the matter?"

"I need to go, I'll call you when I'm checked in."

I clenched the steering wheel and took a deep breath, raising my head to look at the woman who was now on the hood of my car. The very angry woman. Our eyes met through the windshield and for a moment I lost my breath. She was beautiful.

Mentally shaking myself, I turned off the car and got out. My heart was racing. I couldn't believe I'd almost hit someone. I hadn't even seen her.

"I am so sorry. Are you okay? Do you need medical attention?"

The woman made to roll off the hood of the car and I rushed over to help her. I took her hand and everything inside me stilled. *Mine.* The word reverberated through my skull as what felt like an electrical current traveled between our palms.

"Careful," I said softly, my voice rough.

The woman stood up, brushing off her clothing. She was about my age, late forties or early fifties, with a trim, athletic figure. Faded jeans lovingly hugged her slim legs and narrow waist, and her tank top showed toned arms and generous breasts that I was itching to get my hands on. She had thick brown hair that fell past her shoulders in a cascade. Her eyes were chestnut brown, huge in her pale white face, and she had the cutest little button nose. And then there was her mouth...pouty thick lips, slick with some kind of gloss, and pressed together in a frown that told me she wasn't happy.

Oh yeah, probably because I'd hit her with my car.

"Are you okay?" I asked again. "I'm not sure what happened."

Her eyes narrowed in a glare.

"You were driving too fast and too busy talking on your phone to notice I was crossing through this parking space," she told me. "I jumped up on the hood to avoid being crushed."

She pointed at the car in the spot in front of me. There was maybe six inches between the bumper of that car and mine. Jesus. If she hadn't jumped up I might have crushed her. Whoever this woman was, she had good reflexes. I felt sick to my stomach at the idea that I could have seriously hurt her by not paying attention.

"Are you injured?" I asked.

She looked thoughtful and I had the sense she was doing a scan of her body for injuries.

"Probably bruised but nothing's broken, thank God."

"Let me make this right," I said, giving her a smile that had melted a lot of panties in my forty-nine years on this Earth. "Can I buy you dinner later? Or maybe a drink after you check in?"

Her spine snapped straighter, and she gave me a glare that could melt steel.

"Are you seriously hitting on me after you damn near ran me over?"

"Oh. Ah. No," I lied. "I just...what can I do to make it up to you?"

"Watch where you're going next time," she growled. "The next person you try to run over might not be as lucky."

She bent over to pick up the suitcase that she must've dropped when she was evading my car, and I absolutely did not check out her heart-shaped ass. Without another word, she started to walk away at a fast clip.

"At least let me give you my phone number," I said, jogging to catch up with her. "You can call me if you need anything."

She picked up her pace. "Leave me alone, asshole!"

Raising the middle finger of one hand over her shoulder to let me know what she thought of me, she stormed off towards the Main Lodge.

I sat back down in my car, feeling shaken. I couldn't decide if it was because of the near-miss of hitting the woman, or if it was my response to the woman herself. Even angry and flipping me off, there was something about her that called to me. I'd never felt this way about anyone before.

And you let her get away, dumbass, I told myself.

I gathered up my suitcase and headed into the lodge to check in, my pulse still racing. The woman was clearly staying here, so I'd just have to keep a look out for her. If we were meant to be – and I had no doubt that we were – fate would bring her to me again sooner or later.

***

For more of Reed's story – including a cameo by Liz's best friend Renee—check out Summer Wedding, available at select online retailers. For more information visit my website at bit.ly/ AuthorRoseBak[1].

---

1. *https://books2read.com/ap/RDOk1w/Rose-Bak*

Other Books by Rose Bak

Boozy Book Club Series
Beach Reads
Bubbly & Billionaires
Martinis & Mysteries
Bourbon & Bikers
Midlife Madness
Extra Innings
The Good with Numbers Holiday Romance Series
Love Unmasked
The Thanksgiving Scrooge
Maid for Christmas
Countdown to Love
Valentine's Lottery
Christmas Angel
Loving the Holidays Contemporary Romance Series
Dating Santa
New Year's Steve
Independence Dave
Comfort & Joy
Faking It with the Detective
Dropping the Ball
Midlife Crisis Contemporary Romance Series
Summer Wedding
Roasting with Rob
Christmas Punch
Disaster Planning
The Oliver Boys Band Contemporary Romance Series
Until You Came Along
Rock Star Teacher
Rock Star Writer

Rock Star Neighbor
Rock Star Lawyer
Magical Midlife Series
Beltane Magic (prequel)
Love Potion
Psychic Flashes
Halloween Surprise
Giant Love
Bite-Sized Shifters Paranormal Romance Series
Long Distance Wolf
Wolf Doctor
Kat's Dog
Designer Wolf
Wolf Sheriff
Cocktail Wolf
Second Chance Wolf
Runaway Wolf
Holidays with the Shifters Series
Santa's Claws
Bear Humbug
Jingle Bear
Silver Paws
Joy to the Wolf
Lion's Heart
The Diamond Bay Contemporary Romance Series
Brand New Penny
Fresh as a Daisy
Right as Rain
Reunited Series
Together Again
Finding My Baby
King of the Reunion

Standalones
Beach Wedding
Jessie's Girl
Factory Reset
Saving Texas
Texas Christmas
Second Chance to Score
Catch up with these and other stories coming soon. Join my newsletter for more information[1] or follow my author page on your favorite retailer.

---

1.   *https://storyoriginapp.com/giveaways/62ee758e-068f-11eb-904e-c373f6014fe1*

About the Author

Rose Bak has been obsessed with books since she got her first library card at age five. She is a passionate reader with an e-reader bursting with thousands of beloved books.

Although Rose enjoys writing both fiction and nonfiction, romance novels have always been her favorite guilty pleasure, both as a reader and an author. Rose's contemporary romance books focus on strong female characters over thirty-five and the alpha males who love them. Expect a lot of steam, a little bit of snark, and a guaranteed happily ever after.

Rose lives in the Pacific Northwest with her family, and special needs dogs. In addition to writing, she also teaches accessible yoga and loves music. Sadly, she has absolutely no musical talent, so she mostly sings in the shower.

Please sign up for the Rose Bak Romance newsletter[1] to get a free book and keep up to date on all the latest news. You can also follow Rose on Facebook[2], Instagram[3], Twitter[4], Goodreads[5], or Bookbub[6].

---

1. https://storyoriginapp.com/giveaways/62ee758e-068f-11eb-904e-c373f6014fe1

2. https://www.facebook.com/AuthorRoseBak

3. https://www.instagram.com/authorrosebak/

4. https://twitter.com/AuthorRoseBak

5. https://www.goodreads.com/authorrosebak

6. https://www.bookbub.com/authors/rose-bak

Don't miss out!

Visit the website below and you can sign up to receive emails whenever Rose Bak publishes a new book. There's no charge and no obligation.

https://books2read.com/r/B-A-VATM-EIQKC

BOOKS 2 READ

Connecting independent readers to independent writers.

Did you love *Extra Innings*? Then you should read *Beach Reads*[7] by Rose Bak!

She was supposed to be celebrating her sister's birthday, not falling in love with some guy she just met!

When her sister invites her on a girls' weekend to celebrate her fiftieth birthday, Teresa tries her best to get out of it. She's much too busy to take a vacation, let alone spend time with the charming and sexy bartender at the resort they're visiting.

Colin never believed in love at first sight, at least until he set eyes on Teresa. The curvy beauty is everything he's ever wanted in a woman. If he could just convince her to stay...but first, he needs to tell her the truth about who he really is.

It's not just a vacation fling...it's love.

---

7. https://books2read.com/u/3LVKOe

8. https://books2read.com/u/3LVKOe

"Beach Reads" is a prequel novella in the "Boozy Book Club" series. Each story in the series is a steamy standalone featuring a couple over forty-five, a nosy group of matchmaking friends, and a sweet happily ever after that proves anyone can find love later in life.

Read more at https://rosebakenterprises.com/.